DATE DUE

MAR 10 '01			
MAR 23 '01			
APR 05 '01			
JUL 10 '01			
AUG 30 '01			
OCT 18 '01			
NOV 28 '01			
OCT 18 '06			

Grandma's Smile

Elaine Moore

Grandma's Smile

pictures by Dan Andreasen

Lothrop, Lee & Shepard Books   New York

Inquiries should be addressed to Lothrop, Lee & Shepard Books,
a division of William Morrow & Company, Inc.,
1350 Avenue of the Americas, New York, New York 10019.
Printed in Hong Kong
First Edition   1 2 3 4 5 6 7 8 9 10
Library of Congress Cataloging in Publication Data
Moore, Elaine. Grandma's smile / by Elaine Moore; illustrated by Dan Andreasen.
p.   cm.   Summary: Kim's grandmother's smile is the inspiration for the jack-o-lantern
face she draws on her pumpkin at a fall festival.
ISBN 0-688-11075-4. — ISBN 0-688-11076-2 (lib.bdg.)
[1. Grandmothers—Fiction. 2. Pumpkin—Fiction. 3. Harvest festivals—Fiction.
4. Jack-o-lanterns—Fiction.] I. Andreasen,
Dan, ill. II. Title. PZ7.M7832Gt 1995 [E]—dc20 94-23679 CIP AC

For Mom—
E.M.

For my son Brett—
D.A.

"GUESS WHO, GRANDMA?"

"I hope it's Kim," Grandma answers. "I need her to help me haul our last pumpkin to town. There's a jack-o'-lantern contest at the fall festival."

Last summer, Grandma and I grew pumpkins in her garden. I weeded and hoed the little hills. I could hardly wait for the pumpkins to grow, but I never thought they would get this big.

"How will we get it there?" I ask. "That pumpkin is gigantic!"

"I'll show you in a little while. First we need to rake the leaves."

Some of the leaves look like stars. Some look like mittens. Grandma says the red mittens are from her sassafras tree. The gold stars are from the maple. Mmmm, maple syrup.

"There," Grandma says as a squirrel scampers past with an acorn. "We've done enough work for today. Let's wash up and go to the festival."

"Don't forget the pumpkin," I remind Grandma.

I am still wondering how we'll get that giant pumpkin out of the garden when Grandma drives her truck into the field. She gets out and throws an old blanket onto the ground. Then she leans a long, wide board against the end of the truck. Carefully, we roll the pumpkin onto the blanket.

Grandma tells me to stand in the truck. I tug hard with the blanket. Grandma pushes the pumpkin from behind. At last, with one great heave, it bounces into the truck. Oh no, I think. I hope my pumpkin isn't bruised.

Grandma hands me a marking pen. "Write your name at the top," she says.

"Hurray!" I shout. "My pumpkin is going to the fall festival!"

We rumble over the bumpy roads toward the church. Smells of freshly mowed grass and alfalfa tickle my nose. I know we're getting close when I smell farm animals and good things to eat.

"Grandma," I say. "I have never smelled so many different smells all at the same time."

"That's because you've never been to our fall festival before," says Grandma.

Mr. Berg waves his cap to us as we park the truck beside a tent. We head for a group of ladies stirring something in a big black kettle over a fire. Grandma says they are making apple butter.

"Look at those kids over there!" I shout, pulling Grandma's hand. I have never jumped in a haystack before.

Then I look around and sniff. I stop tugging. Doughnuts and hot apple cider!

Grandma takes money out of her coin purse and gives it to me so I can pay the man. He sprinkles sugar on our doughnuts and pours the cider into paper cups. I blow on the steaming cider as we walk slowly toward the haystack. I can hardly wait to get there, but I don't want to spill even a tiny drop.

"Would you like me to hold your cup while you play?" Grandma asks.
I scramble up the bales of hay behind the other girls and boys. When I reach the top, I feel as if I could touch the sun. But when I look down, my stomach starts to tingle.

"Jump!" the boy behind me calls.
I spread my arms and hold my breath.
Whoosh! I land on my back. I jump up and run to stand in line again.

"What's the man doing to his horse?" I ask when Grandma dusts me off.

"That's the blacksmith," Grandma explains. "He's making shoes for the farm horse."

"But Grandma, he's putting them on with a hammer." I am surprised to see the horse stand so still. "Doesn't it hurt?"

"No. Those shoes will protect the horse from sharp stones just like your shoes protect you."

"Can I have a ride when he's finished?" I ask.

"Not on that big horse," Grandma answers. "We'll find some ponies you can ride."

"Ladies and gentlemen. Boys and girls." A voice crackles over the loudspeakers. "Welcome to our fall festival."

We hear music coming from the bandstand. A lady wearing cowboy boots plays the fiddle. We clap our hands and tap our toes. Suddenly Grandma swings me in a circle. We laugh and sing as we do-si-do with the other dancers.

When we stop, I'm out of breath. But not Grandma.

"How about some lunch, with caramel apples for dessert?" she says. "Then we'll see about your ponies. And I still want to check out the crafts."

After my pony ride, Grandma and I take our time in the booths and tents. I see corncob dolls and tiny boats made from walnuts. Grandma chats with a lady who is weaving a purple shawl. She gathered the wool from her lambs. They weren't purple lambs, she says. She tinted the wool with berry juice.

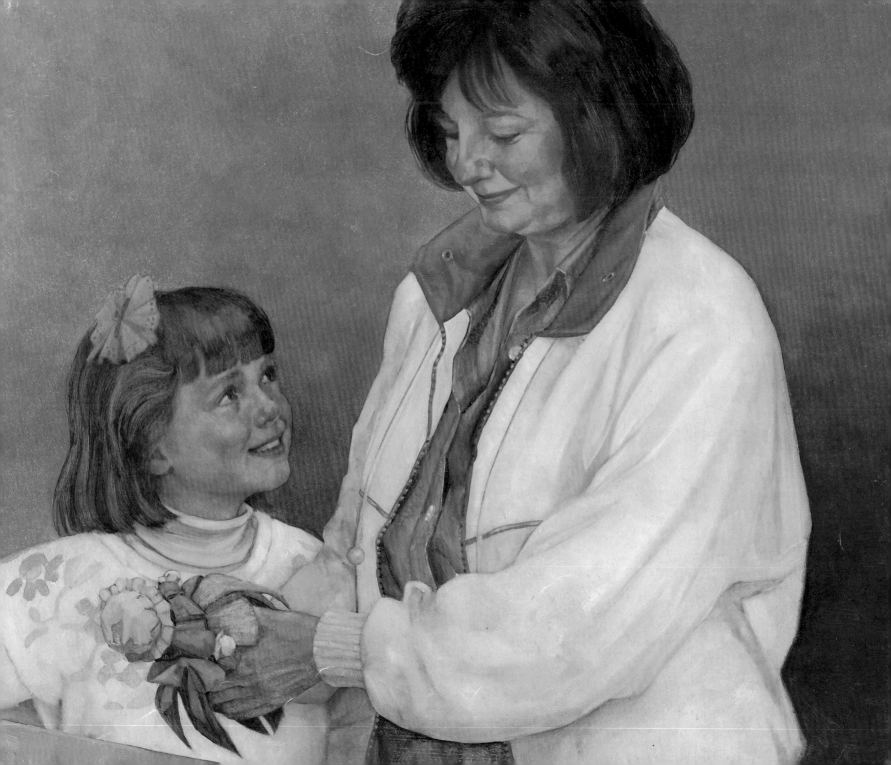

Later, we wander toward the pumpkin tent. Suddenly, I see the back of Grandma's truck is empty.

"Grandma! Our pumpkin is gone!"

Grandma pats my shoulder. "Don't worry, Kim. I asked some friends to move it into the tent while you were playing in the haystack. Let's see if we can find the one that has your name on it."

I don't need to see my name. I know my pumpkin. It's the biggest and the roundest. It's sitting on a table beside a thick black marker and a knife. I look at the shiny blade for a long time.

"Grandma, I don't want my pumpkin to be a jack-o'-lantern."

Grandma squeezes my arm. "Kim, it's time for your pumpkin to be something else—bread and pies and toasted seeds for snacks."

"Not all the seeds. We'll save some seeds to plant next year. Won't we?"

Grandma puts her arms around me. "Of course we will."

"But Grandma," I whisper. "I still don't know what kind of face to draw."

Grandma hands me the black marker. "Why don't you draw your favorite kind of face?" she says.

At first I am not sure. I look at Grandma. Suddenly, I know. I draw the face. Then Grandma carves it.

"That sure is a big smile," she says. "Why, this is probably the happiest jack-o'-lantern in the whole county."

I tap Grandma on her shoulder. "Guess whose smile it is," I say. "Yours."

Grandma answers, "And guess who puts the smile on my face? You."